A Scary Night At The Zoo

Gary Richmond

WORD
Kids!

Dallas • London • Sydney • Singapore

VIEW FROM THE ZOO STORIES are based on the real-life adventures of Gary Richmond, a veteran of the Los Angeles Zoo, minister, counselor, and camp nature speaker. Gary has three children and lives in Chino Hills, California, with his wife, Carol.

C P

Library of Congress Cataloging-in-Publication Data

Richmond, Gary, 1944-
    A scary night in the zoo / by Gary Richmond ; illus-
      trated by Bruce Day.
      p. cm. — (A View from the zoo series)
    Summary: A Christian zookeeper relates an anecdote
about an escaped chimpanzee and draws a parallel
with the lesson that the protection of God and loved
ones is better than running away from home.
    ISBN 0-8499-0742-X : $7.99
    1. Providence and government of God — Juvenile liter-
ature. 2. Interpersonal relations — Religious aspects —
Christianity — Juvenile literature. [1. Christian life.
2. Chimpanzees. 3. Zoos.] I. Day, Bruce, ill. II. Title.
III. Series: Richmond, Gary, 1944- View from the zoo
series.
BT135.R54 1990
242'.62 — dc20   90-12331
                                 CIP
                                 AC

This book is dedicated to my grandson T.J.,
who is a very kind and special boy.

Hi, I'm Gary Richmond, and I'm a zoo keeper. As a zoo keeper, I've learned a lot about God's wonderful animals. At the same time, I've learned a lot about God.

This true story is about a big, mean chimpanzee named Toto and a scary walk in the zoo.

Joey was the zoo security guard. He pulled his car to a quick stop in the aquatics section. (That's where the water animals live). There in the dark shadows was a large, male chimpanzee. The chimp was walking toward the sea lion's area.

Joey had worked at the zoo long enough to know that this was Toto. The zoo had eight chimpanzees. Toto was the worst one to find almost a mile from his cage in the dark. Toto had been a circus chimp and had probably been

treated badly. He was crazy, and you never knew what he would do. He could be gentle and friendly one minute. Then he could be mean and dangerous the next.

Joey rolled up his window and locked all the car doors. Then he picked up his walkie talkie. He clicked it on, and it crackled to life. Joey whispered, "Sam, this is Joey; you there? Over."

Sam said, "Yeah, I'm here. What's up? You sound as if you're looking at a ghost. Over."

"I wish I were," said Joey. "I'm by the chief keeper's shack just below the sea lion area...looking at Toto. Over."

"That sounds like trouble," said Sam. "I'll call the zoo director and the capture team right away. Do your best to keep track of Toto. And keep me posted. And Joey, be really careful. From what I've heard, Toto is bad news."

Joey watched as Toto began walking towards his car. For some reason, Toto stopped near the chief's shack. The truth is, Toto was lost. His cage in the health center had been Toto's home for two years. Without help, he would not be able to find his way back to his cage. Toto didn't know where he was, and he didn't know where else to go. He was scared. In his funny mind, he thought he might be in enemy territory. He probably stayed in the area to be near Joey.

Dr. Gale and the capture team finally arrived. It was very dark. Toto was busy with the sounds and smells of this new place. The zoo's dark green bushes nearly hid Toto's body. Only the sound of his movement told where he was. Dr. Gale told Joey to keep watching Toto. Then he signaled for the capture team to follow him. Once out of Toto's sight, Dr. Gale told the men his plan.

"We can't shoot Toto with the stun gun; it's too dark to know for sure if we hit him," said Dr. Gale. "He might fall into a pool. Or we might miss and scare him so that he escapes from the zoo. Then we'd have to shoot him before he hurt someone in the neighborhood. If any of you have change, give it to me."

The men looked at each other. They wondered what Dr. Gale had in mind. But they knew him well enough not to question him. The change added up to a little less than two dollars. Dr. Gale sighed as he held it in his hand. He gave Bob Spellings fifty cents and told him to get a Coca Cola® from the nearest vending machine.

Then he told the men to go to the zoo's health center. They were to open all the doors and wait there for him and Toto. He was going to try to walk Toto back to his cage. Dr. Gale didn't want Toto to see other people. He thought seeing people might make Toto upset or dangerous.

Bob Spellings came back with the Coke® and handed it to Dr. Gale. He took a sip and gave a 'wish-me-luck' smile. He waited for the men to get out of the area. Then he walked slowly toward Toto. When he got near the escaped chimp, he could see that Toto was nervous. Even in the dark, he could see that Toto was raising up on his back legs. Toto's hair was standing on end. He looked as if he was going to fight.

Dr. Gale spoke softly, "You want something to drink, Toto?"

Toto calmed down and walked slowly forward. He was looking at the cup of Coke® and Dr. Gale. He reached for the man's hand and pulled the cup to his lips. Toto moaned happily at the taste. Then he poured the rest of the Coke® into his mouth.

Dr. Gale was wishing the zoo served larger Coke®s. His plan was to lure Toto from one vending machine to another until they reached Toto's cage. But what if Toto finished everything so quickly? He might not follow Dr. Gale to the next treat. Even worse, Toto might want more. But there would be no more to give him. It never took much to upset Toto. And that was the last thing Dr. Gale wanted to happen in the dark in the middle of the zoo. After all, he was alone. No, he wasn't really alone; there was a crazy circus chimp standing at his side. That chimp was drinking the last drop of Coke® out of a cup that seemed smaller than ever.

Dr. Gale saw the chief keeper's building. He thought he would lock Toto in the building. Then he could get some more money or come up with another plan. So, he offered Toto his hand, and Toto took it. As a young chimp, Toto would have easily held Dr. Gale's hand and followed him. But Dr. Gale didn't know how long Toto might follow as an older chimp. After all, Toto was six times stronger than the doctor.

Dr. Gale removed his keys from his pocket. Then he unlocked the chief keeper's office. He walked into the dark office, hoping Toto would follow. Toto did. It was darker inside than out. Dr. Gale waited until he was sure Toto was completely inside.

Then Dr. Gale made a quick move. He slipped out the door, leaving Toto inside. He slammed the door and locked it. His heart was pounding. Drops of sweat were forming on his forehead. He wiped his forehead and breathed a sigh of relief. Then he tiptoed to look in the window and see if Toto was calmly inside. He shaded his eyes from the glare of the street light. Then he stared into the blackness of the office. He strained his eyes to see Toto, but could not see the chimp.

Suddenly, Dr. Gale felt a hand on his shoulder! He slowly turned to find himself face-to-face with an upset Toto. In a monkey-see monkey-do way, Toto was also shielding his eyes from the glare and staring into the office. He was trying to see what had frightened the doctor.

Dr. Gale gasped and tried to control his voice. He held out his hand to Toto. He quietly said, "Let's go home, Toto."

Toto followed Dr. Gale to the next vending machine. There he bought a small box of Good and Plenty® candies. Toto enjoyed the candies very much. But he would stop, sit down and suck on them; so, progress to the health center was slow. Dr. Gale only had enough money left for one more purchase. And he was not even half way to the center.

Then the wise doctor saw a water fountain. He turned the handle to show Toto how to get a drink. Toto drank lots of water and liked to play with the fountain.

Suddenly a lion roared from its cage nearby. Toto stood
straight up and looked like he would attack. He ran towards
the lion, screaming at the enemy he couldn't see. Then he
looked back at Dr. Gale as if to say, "Well, I guess that takes
care of that." Dr. Gale praised him in a soft voice. He gave
him a Good and Plenty® reward.

Soon the candies ran out; so Dr. Gale made his last purchase — a Payday® candy bar. Toto watched with excitement as a small piece was handed to him. Dr. Gale walked faster now, knowing he was almost out of time. Toto moaned a wait-for-me sound and ran on all four feet to catch up. The Payday® was a favorite choice. The chimp tugged at Dr. Gale's pant leg for another piece. They were making good progress now. It looked as if they would make it to the health center after all.

When they came around the corner at the mountain zebra cage, another scary thing happened. Ed Alonzo, who used to be Toto's keeper, was waiting under a street light. He was watching Dr. Gale's progress with Toto. If Dr. Gale got into trouble, Ed wanted to be there to help. But now Ed was the one in trouble!

When Toto saw Ed under the light, he stood up on his back legs and hooted. Then he dashed away from Dr. Gale at full speed toward terrified Ed. Toto had hurt other people. Ed was sure to be bitten and beaten terribly. So, he braced himself for the attack.

Toto looked mean as he charged closer and closer. Ed
swallowed and prepared for the blow he was about to feel.
At the last possible second, Toto stopped. Then he stood up
in front of Ed to greet him. Toto was just saying hello with a
great deal of excitement.

Seeing a person that Toto knew made him happy. He was tired of the night's adventure. Ed probably reminded him of care and security. Toto reached for Ed's hand, which was still shaking from his fright. So, the last hundred yards were Ed's to cover.

Ed and Toto walked up a narrow path. When they reached the top, they could see the health center. Toto let go of Ed's hand and ran full speed through the health center's door. He walked down the hall to his cage and stood looking through the open door. He seemed to be thinking, "Shall I go in, or shall I stay out?"

At that moment Bill Dickman, a brave but foolish keeper, ran full force into Toto. Bill bumped Toto into his cage and slammed the door behind him. Toto hooted his anger at Bill. But he forgave Bill because he was so happy to be home.

Toto taught me an important lesson: running away from home is not a good idea. It's terrible to be lost and alone.

Just like Dr. Gale helped Toto, God is always ready to help you and me. He gave us nice homes and families. Sometimes we become upset with our families. But we can pray for God to help us understand each other more. And, just as Toto found out: it's always better to be at home with people who love you than all by yourself.